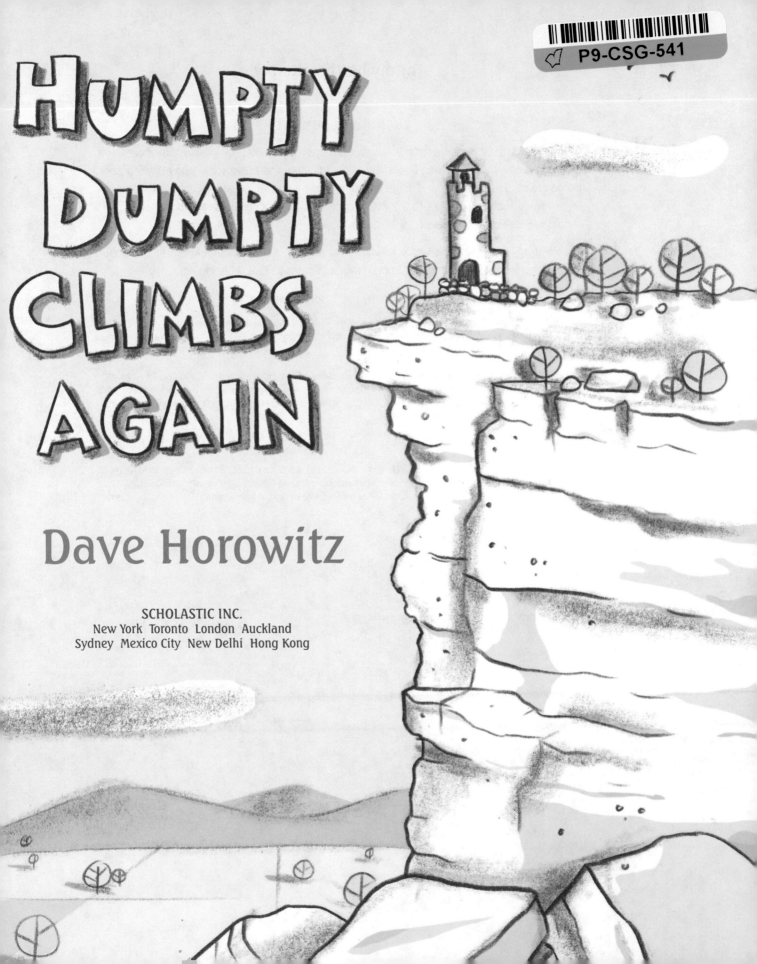

HUMPTY DUMPTY CLIMBS AGAIN

Dave Horowitz

SCHOLASTIC INC.
New York Toronto London Auckland
Sydney Mexico City New Delhi Hong Kong

For my brother, Kenny

– EGGKNOWLEDGMENTS –

It's been said that mountaineering is hours of drudgery punctuated by moments of sheer terror. Let the same be said of making books. Thanks to the following brave souls who played Tenzing Norgay to my Edmund Hillary: First to my editor and friend Nancy Paulsen, who knows exactly what I'm capable of. Thanks to my ever-rugged art team, Cecilia Yung and Richard Amari. Thanks to Sara Kreger for keeping all the pieces together.

Thanks to my agent, Marcia Wernick, who never lets me make a mountain out of a molehill. Special thanks to Elizabeth Cody Kimmel (with apologies to Ernest Shackleton).

And as always, a mountain of thanks to my real heroes, Mom and Dad.

ISBN: 978-0-545-22763-6

12 11 10 9 8 7 6 5 4 3 2   10 11 12 13 14 15/0

Printed in the U.S.A.   40

First Scholastic printing, January 2010

Text set in Seagull
The art was done with black pencil and charcoal on newsprint.
Color was added digitally.

Humpty Dumpty
climbed up a wall...

Humpty Dumpty
had a great fall.

Finally, one of the King's
Horses had the good sense to
call a Doctor.

"Mister Dumpty," said the
Doctor, "you really must be
more careful. I mean—for
Pete's sake—you're an egg!"

Since then, Humpty has not climbed a single wall.

Now All the King's Horses and
All the King's Men make jokes about
Humpty Dumpty.
Whenever they pass his house,
they chant:

Humpty Dumpty
    Sits in a chair,
        He used to climb rocks—
        Today he won't dare.

One day, the Dish went to
visit Humpty Dumpty.

When the Dish arrived,
Humpty Dumpty was sitting
around in his underwear,
watching television.

"Listen, Humpty Dumpty...,"
said the Dish. "This is getting
ridiculous. You used to be such
a brave egg—everybody looked
up to you. Now you just sit
around watching TV?"

"Whatever," said Humpty
Dumpty. "After that great fall
I had, climbing rocks just
seems so silly. I mean what's
the point?"

"If you say so," said the Dish.

And the Dish ran away with
the Spoon.

Humpty Dumpty went back
to watching TV when along
came a Spider.

The Spider dropped down
and frightened Humpty Dumpty
right out of his house.
And there in the middle of
the street stood the once mighty
Humpty Dumpty.

A Little Dog laughed to see
such a sight.

And poor Humpty Dumpty
headed for the hills.

Humpty Dumpty kept walking until he reached the wall. For old times' sake, he climbed up a few big rocks that lay on the bottom.

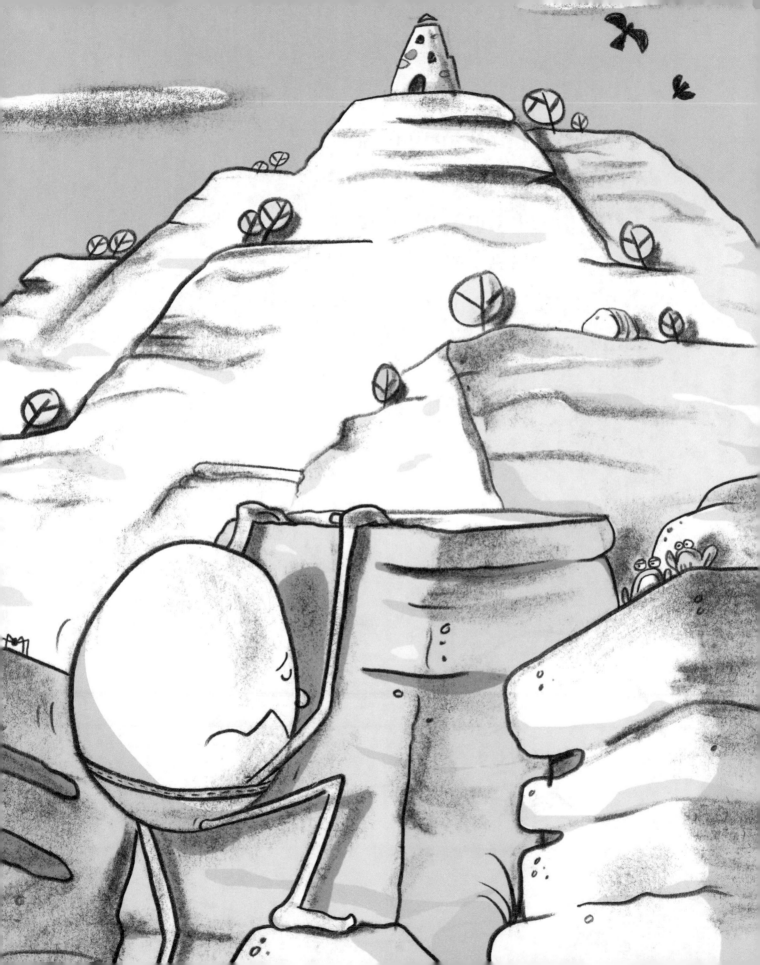

And he found he was not alone.

Oh, *great,* thought Humpty Dumpty. It's All the King's Men— they'll probably make fun of me some more.

But they did not.

All the King's Men had a big problem of their own; the King's favorite Horse, Milt, had gotten stuck way up on the wall.

"The King will have our heads for this," the Men said grimly.

Humpty Dumpty noticed
the climbing equipment
at the Men's feet.
    Without a word he coiled up
their rope, threw it over his
shoulder and . . .

. . . yup, you guessed it—
Humpty Dumpty climbed again.

Yes, Humpty Dumpty
    knew he could fall,
But still, Humpty Dumpty
    climbed up the wall,
For as long as there's trouble
    for Horses and Men,
Good Humpty Dumpty—the egg—
    climbs again.

P.S. And from that day on, Humpty Dumpty never climbed again without the proper safety equipment.

Or pants.